VANESSA BAYER

How Do You Care for a Very Sick Bear?

illustrated by Rosie Butcher

Feiwel and Friends • New York

For my Grandad,
and all the things you dreamed for me.
—R.B.

A Feiwel and Friends Book
An imprint of Macmillan Publishing Group, LLC
175 Fifth Avenue, New York, NY 10010

Our books may be purchased in bulk for promotional, educational, or business use.
Please contact your local bookseller or the Macmillan Corporate and Premium Sales Department at
(800) 221-7945 ext. 5442 or by email at MacmillanSpecialMarkets@macmillan.com.

Library of Congress Cataloging-in-Publication Data
Names: Bayer, Vanessa, 1981-author. | Butcher, Rosie, 1989-illustrator.
Title: How do you care for a very sick bear? / Vanessa Bayer ; illustrated by Rosie Butcher.
Description: First edition. | New York : Feiwel and Friends, 2019. | Summary: Illustrations and
easy-to-read, rhyming text convey advice about what to do when a friend becomes very sick.
Identifiers: LCCN 2018039228 | ISBN 9781250298430 (hardcover)
Subjects: | CYAC: Sick–Fiction. | Friendship–Fiction. | Compassion–Fiction. | Bears–Fiction.
Classification: LCC PZ8.3.B3424 How 2019 | DDC [E]–dc23
LC record available at https://lccn.loc.gov/2018039228

Book design by Rebecca Syracuse
Feiwel and Friends logo designed by Filomena Tuosto
The artwork was created with digital brushes in Corel Painter 12.
1 3 5 7 9 10 8 6 4 2
First edition, 2019

mackids.com

For Gwen, Lissy, Kitty, Ariel, Jenny, Julie, Jonah, Mom, Dad, and so many others for taking such good care of me.

—V.B.

You and your friend Bear
are a very nice pair.

You play,
you laugh.

You talk,
you dream.

You know each other so well.

You and your friend Bear
are an excellent pair.

But if your friend gets sick and can't do all the things that you two love to do . . .

You may wonder—

How do you care for a very sick bear?

You can call her, or visit, and tell her the news. You can bring her cards, and books, and things to do.

Games are fun.
Snacks are fun, too.

Your friend Bear might look
different; she might have less hair.
She might be too tired to play.

And that might feel scary.

Your friend Bear
might feel scared, too.

But seeing you and having you
near helps her feel better.

And it helps you, too.

Because you and your friend
Bear are a *wonderful* pair.

There may be times
your friend seems sad.

You can ask her how she's feeling
or if there's anything she needs.

If she wants to talk, you're
the perfect friend to listen.

If she wants to be alone, you'll find another time to play.

She is still your Bear,

and you are hers.

You and your friend Bear
are a marvelous pair.

Author's Note

When I was fifteen, I was diagnosed with leukemia and was treated for about two and a half years. Something that really made a difference during that time was being surrounded by friends. When I was too sick to go to school, they sent me cards and called me on the phone and visited me. We'd sit on my bed and I'd get updates on all the latest buzz at school, or if I was up to it we'd go for a walk and talk about our favorite TV shows, or what we wanted to be someday, or who we had a crush on. Sometimes we laughed and sometimes we cried.

It was hard being sick. There were times I felt uncomfortable or scared or sad, and I knew that my friends were probably feeling that way, too. But having them by my side—and knowing they were there for me—really made me feel wonderful.

Now as an adult, I've noticed that a lot of people (even adults!) don't know what to do when a friend becomes ill or is dealing with some other kind of trauma. That's why I wanted to write this book. Because having been on the other side of it, my advice is simple: The way that you care for a very sick bear—or B(ay)ear or anyone, really!—is to be there for them.